IF HALLOWEEN Could Be EVERY DAY

by
Sierra Gullickson

Illustrated by
Eric M. Strong

To my hauntingly handsome husband, Cody

Part of the Read Sing Laugh book series
Copyright © 2019 by Sierra Gullickson
Printed in the U.S.A.

In Kindergarten I was asked
to choose my favorite day.
A day I could live in forever.
How do I choose what to say?

REAL HEROES

Now I know what you are thinking—
the choice is simple, plain and clear.
You'd have to choose your birthday
with endless presents far and near.

Fourth of July is up on my list
with fireworks, pool parties, and a parade,
but the only way I could take that miserable heat
is in the ocean as a mermaid.

But to have no snack time or recess and not get to see my friends makes me oh so sad.
I want to see my teacher again!

The day I get to hide from friends
and jump out yelling "BOO!"
At first their faces frightened
until they see it's you!

We go to the local pumpkin patch
to pick out the best pumpkin.
I skip through the vines, can't wait to get home.
Let the jack-o-lantern carving begin!

I pick out a haunting face for my pumpkin.
My dad presses the knife in with all his might.
Slitted eyes, sharp teeth, and lips curled in a snarl
flicker in the candlelight.

My brother helps me build
our own haunted house in the storage shed.
We deck it out with spiders and ghouls,
strobe lights and a fake skeleton head.

ENTER
IF YOU
DARE!

Getting to dress up as anything I want
is what I would love the most.
I would be a beautiful princess
and dress my cat up as a ghost.

I host a thrilling party
where my friends think, "Do I dare try this food?"
with smoking dry ice and ketchup as blood
that really sets the eerie mood.

The feast includes bloody-hand meatloaf
and monster sandwiches with curly-fry hair,
peanut butter spider cookies,
and marshmallow ghosts floating in mid-air.

My friends show up to my party
in the most amazing costumes.
There's a vampire, a mummy, a six-legged cow,
even a zombie bride and groom.

The night wears on, my legs get tired.
How many houses can there be?
My feet are dragging, my pumpkin's so heavy.
"Mom, take me home to my cat," I plead.

This glamming up and scaring people
is fine until hour two or three.
I'm tired of this tiara and clumsy dress.
I just want to go back to being me!

The suspense is gone knowing everything's fake.
There is nothing scary to fear.
I'm getting sick of Halloween.
I'm instead ready for a little cheer.

I wouldn't want to miss birthdays or weekends
or any days in between.
I realize every day is special,
not just Halloween.

If Halloween Could Be Every Day Song
By Sierra Gullickson

If Halloween could be every day
I'd shout out "Boo" in a spooky way
The frights, the haunts
Dress-up however I want
If Halloween could be every day

We'd give our pumpkin a haunting face
And set it out in the perfect place
Big eyes, sharp teeth that glow in the night
Curled lips flicker in the candlelight

If Halloween could be every day
I'd shout out "Boo" in a spooky way
The frights, the haunts
Dress-up however I want
If Halloween could be every day

We'd build a haunted house in our shed
Deck it out with ghouls and a skeleton head
Some great big spiders crawling up in their web
Would give friends goosebumps and add to the dread

If Halloween could be every day
I'd shout out "Boo" in a spooky way
The frights, the haunts
Dress-up however I want
If Halloween could be every day

I'd have the best party I must confess
My cat dressed as a ghost and I, a princess
I serve friends food that gives them a fright
Then we trick-or-treat til the end of the night

If Halloween could be every day
I'd shout out "Boo" in a spooky way
The frights, the haunts
Dress-up however I want
If Halloween could be every day

I'm tired of walking
My feet hurt bad
If Halloween ended
I wouldn't be too sad

Forget the fear
Instead I want cheer
Maybe Halloween should be only one day

Enjoy these spookalicious Halloween recipes

Peanut Butter Spider Cookies

1 peanut butter cookie mix
1/2 cup sugar
36 peanut butter cups
1/2 cup milk chocolate chips
1/4 cup white chocolate chips

Preheat oven to 375°F. Prepare cookie mix as directed. Shape dough into 36 balls, about 1 1/2 inch wide, and then roll in sugar. Bake for 8-10 minutes or until edges are light golden brown and top of cookie shows cracking. Unwrap peanut butter cups. Place hot cookies on wax paper and gently push in one peanut butter cup upside down into center of cookie. Let melt slightly, and then place two white chocolate chips into warm peanut butter cup as eyes. Melt milk chocolate chips on stovetop or microwave slowly and stirring constantly, then transfer to a ziplock bag. Cut off a small corner of the bag. Use as a decorating tip to squeeze chocolate onto cookie, putting three chocolate legs on the sides of each cookie and two dots on the white chocolate chips as eye pupils. Let cool completely before moving.

Bloody-hand Meatloaf

Meatloaf:
2 lbs. ground beef
1 egg
3/4 cup milk
1 cup shredded cheese
1/2 cup oatmeal
1/2 cup chopped onion
1 Tbsp. worcestershire sauce

Sauce:
2/3 cup ketchup
1/2 cup brown sugar
1 1/2 tsp. mustard

Preheat oven to 350°F. Combine meatloaf ingredients in a large bowl. Place on greased cookie sheet (I like to cover the cookie sheet with tin foil for easier clean up. Spray tin foil with cooking spray). Form into the shape of a hand. Don't make the fingers too narrow otherwise they may burn easily. Combine sauce ingredients in a small bowl, and spread sauce over meatloaf. Bake meatloaf for one hour. Enjoy!

Monster chicken Sandwiches

4 chicken patties
4 hamburger buns
4 slices of Swiss cheese
Lettuce leaves
8 green olives
Toothpicks
Curly fries

Bake chicken patties and curly fries as directed on packaging. Cut small triangles out of one edge of each slice of cheese to make it look like teeth. Immediately after taking the chicken patties out of the oven while on cooking tray, place one slice of cheese on each chicken patty and allow to melt slightly so that cheese lays over the chicken. Stack chicken, cheese, and lettuce on the bun. Poke a toothpick in an olive and stick into the top of the bun for an eye. Repeat for second eye. Push in curly fries in the top of the bun behind the olives for hair.

Made in the
USA
Lexington, KY